Jessica Souhami studied textile design at the
Central School of Art and Design. In 1980 she formed
Mme Souhami & Co, a travelling puppet company using colourful
shadow puppets with musical accompaniment and a storyteller. Her books
for Frances Lincoln include *The Leopard's Drum*, *Old MacDonald*, *Rama and the
Demon King*, two volumes of *Silly Rhymes: One Potato, Two Potato* and
Mother Caught a Flea, and *The Black Geese*, written by Alison Lurie.
Jessica Souhami works in collaboration with
book designer Paul McAlinden.

The story of the Old Woman and the Pumpkin

NO DINNER!

Jessica Souhami

Frances Lincoln

This story is based on a popular folk tale,
The Old Woman and the Pumpkin, told across the Indian subcontinent

No Dinner copyright © Frances Lincoln Limited 1999
Text, illustrations and design copyright © Jessica Souhami 1999

First published in Great Britain in 1999 by
Frances Lincoln Children's Books, 4 Torriano Mews,
Torriano Avenue, London NW5 2RZ
www.franceslincoln.com

This edition published 2008

British Library Cataloguing in Publication Data available on request

ISBN 978-1-84507-818-8

Set in ITC Garamond and Rockwell Bold Condensed

Printed in China

3 5 7 9 8 6 4 2

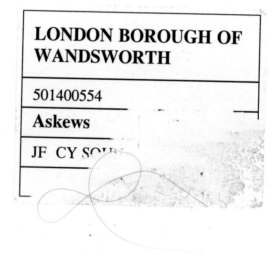

There was once an old woman who lived at the edge of a big forest with her little dog. She was so bent and frail that she was nothing but skin and bone.

She longed to visit her granddaughter who lived on the other side of the forest. But the forest was full of fierce, hungry animals.

Nevertheless, one day she said goodbye to her little dog
and set off with her walking stick to cross the forest,
sure that she would be home again soon, happy and fat.
She walked slowly, tapping with her stick…

tagook…tagook…tagook…when suddenly…

"Very well," said the old woman. "But look at me.
I'm all skin and bone. I'm on my way to my
granddaughter's house where I'll get nice and fat.
   Why don't you eat me on my way home?"

"All right," said the wolf, **"but don't be too long.
I'm hungry!"**

   And the wolf disappeared. And on she walked and
her stick went tagook…tagook…tagook….

   But then…

"Very well," said the old woman. "But look at me.
I'm all skin and bone. I'm on my way to my
granddaughter's house where I'll get nice and fat.
Why don't you eat me on my way home?"

"All right," said the bear, **"but don't be too long.
I'm hungry!"** And the bear disappeared.
And on walked the old woman and her stick went
tagook…tagook…tagook…until…

"Boo!"

Out jumped a tiger.

"Old woman, I'm going to eat you up!"

"Very well," said the old woman. "But look at me. I'm all skin and bone. I'm on my way to my granddaughter's house where I'll get nice and fat.

Why don't you eat me on my way home?"

"All right," said the tiger, **"but don't be too long. I'm hungry!"** And the tiger disappeared. And on she walked and her stick went tagook...tagook...tagook... until at last she reached her granddaughter's house.

Her granddaughter was surprised and happy to
see her. She gave her grandmother the most delicious
food and the old woman ate and ate and ate.

"Granny," said her granddaughter at last, "if you eat
one more thing, you will burst."

The old woman laughed.

"That's true," she said, "and now I'm nice and fat
the animals in the forest will want to eat me.
How can I get home safely?"

"Don't worry, Granny," said her granddaughter,
"I have a plan. Here is a huge, red pumpkin. I've cut
off the top and scooped out the middle so you will fit
inside. Then you can roll home through the forest and
the animals won't see you."

And she helped her grandmother into the pumpkin
shell where she was nice and snug.

She put on the lid and gave it a gentle push,
and it rolled along galook...galook...galook....
Very soon...

Out jumped the tiger.

"Pumpkin, have you seen a little old woman?"

"No," called the old woman from inside the pumpkin. "I'm just a pumpkin rolling home. I haven't seen an old woman."

"Bother!" said the tiger. **"No dinner."**

And the pumpkin rolled on galook...galook...galook....

But then...

Out jumped the bear.

"Pumpkin, have you seen a little old woman?"

"No," called the old woman from inside the pumpkin.

"I'm just a pumpkin rolling home. I haven't seen an old woman."

"Bother!" said the bear. **"No dinner."**

And the pumpkin rolled on galook...galook...galook... until...

Out stepped the wolf.

"Pumpkin, have you seen a little old woman?"

"No," called the old woman from inside the pumpkin. "I'm just a pumpkin rolling home. I haven't seen an old woman."

"**Bother!**" said the wolf. "**No dinner.**"

But, just as the pumpkin was about to roll on…
"Just a minute," said the wolf.
"I've never heard a TALKING pumpkin."

And he lifted the lid from the top of the pumpkin
and out popped the old woman's head.

"Very well," she said, "you can eat me now. But first, I have to tell you that I didn't get nice and fat at my granddaughter's house. Not at all. I'm still just skin and bone."

"Show me," said the wolf.
"Put out your leg for me to feel."

And the crafty old woman poked out not her leg but her walking stick, and the wolf felt that.

"Bother!" he said.
"Hard as bone.
Not nice and fat at all.
BOTHER! BOTHER! BOTHER!
NO DINNER!"

And he pushed the pumpkin in disgust.

And the pumpkin rolled along galook, galook, galook, until it reached her house on the far side of the forest.

The clever old woman got out of the pumpkin shell, happy and fat and safe. And her little dog ran to meet her, wagging his tail.

And that is the end of the story.